William Henry Rideing

Thackeray's London

His Haunts and the Scenes of his Novels

William Henry Rideing

Thackeray's London
His Haunts and the Scenes of his Novels

ISBN/EAN: 9783337046828

Printed in Europe, USA, Canada, Australia, Japan

Cover: Foto ©Andreas Hilbeck / pixelio.de

More available books at **www.hansebooks.com**

William Makepeace Thackeray.

WILLIAM H. RIDEING

𝕿𝖍𝖆𝖈𝖐𝖊𝖗𝖆𝖞'𝖘 𝕷𝖔𝖓𝖉𝖔𝖓

HIS HAUNTS AND THE SCENES
OF HIS NOVELS

ILLUSTRATED

BOSTON
CUPPLES, UPHAM AND COMPANY
The Old Corner Bookstore
283 Washington St.
1885.

THACKERAY'S LONDON.

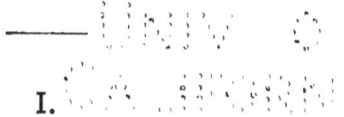

I.

THACKERAY does not give the same opportunities for the identification of his scenes as Dickens. The elaboration with which the latter localizes his characters, and the descriptive minutiæ with which he makes their haunts no less memorable than themselves, are not to be found in the works of the author of *Vanity Fair*. No faculty was stronger in Dickens, or of more service to him, than his power of word-painting. He reproduces the objects

by which the persons he describes are surrounded with a fidelity which would be
tedious, if it were not relieved by the humor
which humanizes bricks, and imparts a
grotesque sort of sensibility to articles of
furniture; and it is not easy to think of any
of his leading characters without being
reminded of the neighborhoods in which
they played their parts.

Thackeray, on the contrary, is not topo-
graphical. The briefest mention of a street
suffices with him, and it is the character,
not the locality, which has permanence in
the reader's mind. Every feature of Becky
Sharp is remembered with a vividness
which disassociates her with fiction ; but
the situation of the little house in which
the unfortunate Rawdon finally discovers
her duplicity, in the famous scene with the
Marquis of Steyne, escapes the memory.
When the book is no longer fresh to him,

the reader may recollect that after her mar-
riage she went to live in Mayfair, and
may picture to himself a small, fashionable
dwelling in that aristocratic neighbourhood;
but he cannot remember that the author
places it in Curzon street, nor that the
Sedleys lived in Russell Square, Philip in
Old Parr street, and Colonel Newcome in
Fitzroy Square.

We have one example in Thackeray of
the grotesquely humorous descriptive power
of which Dickens was a master. It hits at
the absurd nomenclature of modern London
suburbs, where every box of a house has
some high-sounding name of the sort which
ornaments the fiction of the " Chamber-
maid's Companion," and it describes the
neighbourhood into which the Sedleys
moved after their failure—" St. Adelaide
Villa, Anna Maria Road, West, where the
houses look like baby houses; where the

people looking out of the first floor windows must infallibly, as you think, sit with their feet in the parlors below; where the shrubs in the little gardens in front bloom with a perennial display of little children's pinafores, little red socks, caps, etc. *(polyandria polygenia);* whence you hear the sound of jingling spinets and women singing; and whither, of an evening, you see city clerks plodding wearily."

The fanciful supposition that persons in the upper stories must have their legs on the lower floor is richly characteristic of the manner in which Dickens would have indicated the smallness of the houses. It is a touch of that kind of humour which distinguishes all the work of that author, and which was one of his most serviceable resources; it gives facial expression to inanimate objects, and, as we have said, it individualizes the haunts of his characters

no less than the characters themselves,
But it is so rare in Thackeray that the
exhibition of it in this fragment strikes
us, as the lurid style of the earlier writings
of Lord Lytton would do if we were to
find a passage from them interpolated
among the confiding garrulities of *Vanity
Fair.*

It was not that Thackeray lacked the
power of observation in the direction of
externals,—though he certainly did not
possess it in the same degree as Dickens
—nor that his characters were airy visions
to him, requiring no other habitation than
the chambers of his brain ; they were
indeed flesh and blood to him, and Miss
Thackeray has told a friend of the writer's,*
how, in her walks with her father, he would
point out the very houses in which they
lived. The difference was principally one

* Mr. R. R. Bowker.

of method. Thackeray's was the classic
stage—a dais with a drapery of green baize,
before the time of scenery. Dickens's was
the modern stage, with lime-lights, trap-
doors, and elaborate " sets."

II.

THOUGH his other scenes are misty, no reader of Thackeray who engages in a search for the places which he describes is likely, however, to overlook the Charterhouse, the ancient foundation to which he refers again and again, dwelling on it with many fond reminiscences. It is the school in which he himself was educated, and he has associated three generations of his characters with it. Thomas Newcome received instruction here, also his son Clive, with Pendennis, Osborne, and Philip of the second generation, after whom came Rawdon Crawley's little son and young George

Osborne; and, finally, the dear old Colonel,
when broken down and weary, joined the
poor brethren who are pensioners of the
institution, and within its monastic walls
cried *Adsum* as he heard a voice summon-
ing him to the everlasting peace. Occasionally it is called Slaughter-house, once
or twice " Smiffle" (after the boys' way of
pronouncing Smithfield, where it is situ-
ated); but in Thackeray's later works he
generally speaks of it as Grayfriars or
Whitefriars.

" It had been," he says in *Vanity
Fair,* "a Cistercian convent in old days
when the Smith field, which is contiguous to it, was a tournament ground.
Obstinate heretics used to be brought
thither, convenient for burning hard by.
Henry the Eighth seized upon the monastery and its possessions, and hanged and
tortured some of the monks who would not

OLD CHAPEL, WITH THE FOUNDER'S TOMB—CHARTER-HOUSE

accommodate themselves to the pace of his reform. Finally, a great merchant bought the house and land adjoining, in which, with the help of other wealthy endowments of land and money, he established a famous foundation hospital for old men and children. An extra school grew round the old, almost monastic foundation, which subsists still with its middle-age costume and usages ; and all Christians pray that it may flourish.

" Of this famous house some of the greatest noblemen, prelates and dignitaries in England, are governors ; and as the boys are very comfortably lodged, fed and educated, and subsequently inducted to good scholarships at the University, and livings in the Church, many little gentlemen are devoted to the ecclesiastical profession from their tenderest years, and there is considerable emulation to procure nomina-

tions for the foundation. It was originally
intended for the sons of poor and deserving
clerics and laics ; but many of the noble
governors of the institution, with an en-
larged and rather capricious benevolence,
selected all sorts of objects for their bounty.
To get an education for nothing, and a
livelihood and profession assured, was so
excellent a scheme, that some of the richest
people did not disdain it ; and not only the
great men's relations, but great men themselves, sent their sons to profit by the
chance. Right reverend prelates sent their
own kinsmen as the sons of their clergy,
while on the other hand some great noblemen did not disdain to patronize the
children of their confidential servants, so
that a lad entering this establishment had
every variety of youthful society where-
with to mingle."

As a rule, however, the boys belong

to the upper classes, and an education
obtained at Charterhouse is scarcely less
of a social distinction than the much
coveted and costly preparation of Eton,
Harrow, or Winchester. The history of
the school is full of brilliant names, and
among its scholars have been Joseph
Addison, Richard Steele, Isaac Barrow,
General Havelock, Sir William Blackstone,
Lord Chief Justice Ellenborough, Lord
Liverpool, John Wesley and George Grote.

It is possible that one may know London
intimately, and yet be ignorant of the situation of the Charterhouse. Smithfield is
out of the way of the main lines of traffic :
it is a squalid neighbourhood, north of
Ludgate Hill, and it retains its ancient
characteristics more than almost all other
parts of the great city,—which has been so
modernized that Cheapside looks like a
slice of Broadway, and once shabby Fleet

Street is showing all sorts of ornamental
fronts. It has in it many solemn brick houses
of a blackish purple, with glowing roofs of
red tiles; smaller buildings of an earlier
period, with high peaked gables and over-
lapping second stories; sequestred alleys,
and courts bearing queer names, and many
curious little shops.

One of the most direct approaches to
it is through the Old Bailey from Ludgate
Hill. On this route we pass the austere
granite of Newgate Prison and also Pye
Corner, where as the sign-board of a
public house tells us, the great fire of
1666 ended, after burning from the 2nd to
the 10th of September; we also pass
Cock Lane, famous for its ghost, and the
quaintest of old London churches, St. Bartholomew the Great, which is hemmed in
and partly extinguished by the surrounding
houses, that hide all but its smoked and

patched tower, and a few square feet of
grass, which is justifiably discouraged in
its want of sunshine and space ; thence our
path is by the extensive buildings of St.
Bartholomew's Hospital, about which there
is a morbid activity in the flow of officials
and visitors, most of the latter being slat-
ternly and anxious-looking women, with
babies and baskets on their arms, and from
the Hospital we cross the street, and so
through the new cattle market, which fills
the space once occupied by the pens, and
covers the spot whence the souls of many
martyrs have passed in flame from the
stake to heaven.

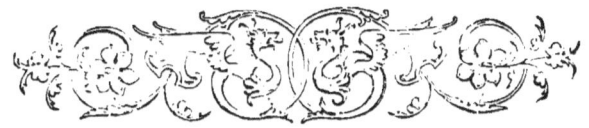

III.

THE buildings form an irregular cluster spread over a prodigal area, and isolated by a wall of brick and stone which many London fogs and long days of yellow weather have reduced to the dismalest of colors. None of them are lofty ; some of them are of granite, and others of brick, upon which age has cast a smoky mantle. They are separated by wide courts and winding passages ; and when I was there in the Easter vacation these open spaces were vacant, and the brisk twittering of the sparrows was the only sound that came from them. The quiet seemed all the greater, inasmuch as all

around the walls is a busy neighbourhood,
full of traffic and voices. The courts are
for the most part paved with small cobble-
stones, and are cleanly swept ; but some
of them are grassy—grassy in the dingy
and feeble way of London vegetation.
These buildings look as sad as they are
old ; to the juvenile imagination the high
walls and the severe architecture must be
sharply distressing, and many a boy has
felt his heart sink with misgiving as, for
the first time, he has been driven through
the old gate-way, to be placed as a scholar
on Thomas Sutton's* famous foundation.

* The school was founded by Thomas Sutton,
a rich merchant, in 1611. The buildings which
are mostly of the 16th Century, had been used until
the Reformation, as a monastery of Carthusian
monks. "Charterhouse" is a corruption of Char-
treuse, and the scholars still call themselves Carthusians.

At this old gate-way, one day, I saw a
very feeble old gentleman, strangely dressed
in a scarlet waistcoat and bright blue trow-
sers, a brass-buttoned coat, and a high silk
hat. He was very small and very weak,
moving slowly with the help of a stick, and
coughing painfully behind his pocket hand-
kerchief. To my question as to the ad-
mission of strangers, he said, quaveringly :
"If you are a patron, you may see the
buildings, but you had better ask the
janitor ; there he is. I," he added, with
some hesitation, "I am one of the poor
brethren."

The old head bowed down with years
and sorrow, the white hair, the troublesome
cough, the courteous amiability of manner,
reminded me of Colonel Newcome—Codd
Newcome, as the boys began to call him ;
and, indeed, this old gentleman had been
a captain in the Queen's service, as the

janitor afterward told us, though he was not as stately nor as handsome as the dear old Colonel was. None of the celebrities of Charterhouse possesses the same vivid interest, the same hold upon our sympathies, the same command of the affections, as the brave, high-minded, large-hearted old soldier, who sacrificed all he had in the world to keep his honour spotless, and to shield others from misery.

As the janitor took us from hall to hall in the dark, monastic buildings, Colonel Newcome was constantly before us, and his figure, even more than that of Thackeray himself, filled our minds, and made us feel kindly to the old pensioners who were sunning themselves at the doors of their rooms, or were gathered in a quiet corner of one of the courts, chatting or reading.

The pensioners, of whom there are eighty,

remain in the old buildings, in which each
of them has a sitting-room and a bed-room,
with a servant to wait upon him. Their
table is a common one, in a grand old
dining-hall, and twice a day they don their
gowns to go to service in the little chapel,
to thank God for his manifold blessings
and mercies. But the boys have been removed since 1870 to a magnificent new
school at Godalming, Surrey, thirty-four
miles away from London fogs and the
crowds of Smithfield, and they have taken
nearly all the relics of Thackeray with
them, including the little bed in which he
slept while a scholar. Their part of the
buildings is now occupied by the Merchant
Taylors' School, which has added a large
new schoolroom to the square. The ground
is immensely valuable, and from an eco-
nomic point of view it seems a waste to
devote it to the obsolete buildings which

fill the greater part of it. Soon, no doubt, another home will be found for the poor brethren, and when commerce takes possession of Charterhouse Square, one of the most interesting piles in London town will disappear.*

The cleanliness and orderliness which leave no scrap of waste or wisp of straw or ridge of dust visible in the approach have also swept up every part of the interior; and though the smoke and dust have taken a tenacious hold, the charwoman's

* Several relics of Thackeray are preserved in the new school at Godalming, including some pen and ink sketches made by him, and five volumes containing all the existing MS. of *The Newcomes*. The MS. is written partly in his own hand, partly in the hand of Miss Anne Thackeray (now Mrs. Ritchie), and partly in another hand. Several stones on which some of the old scholars, including Thackeray, carved their names, have also been removed from the old school in London to the new one.

besom and scrubbing-brush have been
vigorously applied. The buildings look
quite as old as they are. The oaken wainscoting is the deepest brown ; the balusters
and groining are massive and carved ; the
tapestries are indistinct and phantasmal,
like faded pictures, and the walls are like
those of a fortress. It is easy in these
surroundings to conjure up visions of the
middle ages.

The site of the dormitories of the Charterhouse boys is now occupied by the new
school-room of the Merchant Taylors ;
but looking upon it is a dusky cloister,
once given to the prayerful meditations
of the friars, which in Thackeray's time
and later was used for games of ball ;
the gloom is everywhere. The ghosts of
the silent brothers seem fitter tenants than
the boys with shining faces and ringing
voices. There are narrow, suspicious-look-

ing passages, and heavily-barred, irresistible
oaken doors. But these corridors and bar-
riers against the unwelcome lead into several apartments of truly magnificent size and
faded splendour. The dining-hall of the
poor brethren has wainscoting from twelve
to twenty feet high, a massively groined
roof, a musicians' gallery with a carved
balustrade, and a large fire-place framed
in ornamental oak, over which the Sutton
arms are emblazoned ; while at the end of
the room is a portrait of the founder,
dressed in a flowing gown and the suffo-
catingly frilled collar of his time. Parallel
to this, and accessible by a low door, is
the dining-hall of the gown boys, a long,
narrow room, with a very low ceiling, high
wainscoting, a knotty floor, insufficient windows, and another large fire-place inclosed
by an elaborate mantel-piece of oak. Here
almost side by side, these boys with life

untried before them and the old men well-
nigh at their journey's end, ate the bread
provided for them by their common bene-
factor, and joined voices in thanksgiving;
here still the old pensioners assemble, and
in trembling voices murmur grace over the
provision made for them. Upstairs there
is a banqueting-hall, which is not inferior
in sombre grandeur to that of the poor
brothers, and was once honoured by the
presence of Queen Elizabeth. It also is
wainscoted and groined, and hung with
tapestries, out of which the pictures have
nearly vanished. The fire-place is the
finest of all, and above it some hazy paint-
ings are lost in the shadow.

Thackeray was one of the foundation
scholars, and lived in the school, and wore
a gown. He was, from all accounts, an
average boy, undistinguished by industry
or precocious ability. He was very much

like many of Dr. Birch's little friends : a
simple honest, and sometimes mischievous
lad. Though he was never elected orator
or poet, he wrote parodies, and was clever
with a pencil, which he used with no little
fancy and humour. The margins of books
and scraps of paper of all kinds were
covered with sketches, most of them cari-
catures ; and it is said to have been a
familiar thing to see the artist surrounded
by an admiring crowd of his school-fellows,
while he developed, with grotesque extra-
vagance and never-failing effect, the outlines
of some juvenile hero or some notability of
history. The head master of the school
was severe, and as Thackeray was very
sensitive, it is supposed that his school
days were not of the happiest. But he
bore the old foundation no ill-will ; who,
indeed, shall ever do it more honor than
he has done ?

Only a few weeks before his death, Thackeray was present on Founder's Day. He sat in his usual back seat in the old chapel. He went thence to hear the oration in the governor's room, and, as he walked up to the orator with his contribution, was received with hearty applause. At the banquet afterward, he sat at the side of his old friend and school-mate John Leech ; and Thackeray it was who, on that occasion proposed the toast of "The Charterhouse."

Taking us through the grounds by the way of Wash-house Court, a quadrangle of very old and smoky buildings, which were attached to the original monastery, the janitor conducted us into the cool and quiet cloister which leads into the chapel. Here is the handsome memorial of the Carthusians slain in the wars, and on the walls is a commemorative tablet to Thackeray.

CLOISTER LEADING INTO THE CHAPEL, WITH THE MEMORIAL TABLETS
OF THACKERAY AND LEECH

Next to Thackeray's is a similar tablet to the memory of Leech.

The little chapel is much as it was in their time and long before. The founders' tomb, with its grotesque carvings, monsters, heraldries, still darkles and shines with the most wonderful shadows and lights, as Thackeray described it. There, in marble effigy, lies Fundator Noster in his ruff and gown, awaiting the great examination day. Just in front of this elaborate monument, Thackeray himself used to sit when a boy. The children are present no more; but yonder, twice a day, sit the pensioners of the hospital, listening to the prayers and the psalms,—four-score of the old reverend black gowns. The custom of the school was that, on the twelfth of December, the head gown boy should recite a Latin oration; and, though the scholars are removed to Godalming, the ceremony is

perpetuated. Many old Carthusians attend
this oration ; after which they go to chapel
and hear a sermon, which is followed by a
dinner, at which old condisciples meet, old
toasts are given, and speeches are made.
The reader has surely not forgotten how
Pendennis, himself a Grayfriars boy, came
to the festival one day quite unaware of his
friend's presence.

"The pensioners were in their benches,
the boys in their places, with young
fresh faces and shining white collars.
We oldsters, be we ever so old," Pendennis has written, "become boys again as
we look at that old familiar tomb, and think
how the seats are altered since we were
here, and how our doctor—not the present
doctor, the doctor of *our* time—used to sit
yonder, and his awful eye used to frighten
us shuddering boys on whom it lighted ;
and how the boy next us *would* kick our

shins during service time, and how the
monitor would cane us afterwards, because
our shins were kicked. Yonder sit forty
cherry-cheeked boys, thinking about home
and holidays to-morrow. Yonder sit the
pensioners coughing feebly in the twilight.
Is Codd Ajax alive you wonder ?—the Cistercian lads called these old gentlemen
Codds, I know not wherefore—but is old
Codd Ajax alive I wonder ? or Codd
soldier ? or kind old Codd gentleman ? or
has the grave closed over them ?

" A plenty of candles light up this chapel,
and this scene of age and youth, and early
memories, and pompous death. How
solemn the well-remembered prayers are,
here uttered again in the place where in
childhood we used to listen to them. How
beautiful and decorous the rite, how noble
the ancient words of the supplications
which the priest utters. and to which gene-

rations of fresh children, and troops of
by-gone seniors have cried Amen! under
those arches! The service for Founder's
Day is a special one; one of the Psalms
selected being the thirty-seventh, and we
hear :— 23. 'The steps of a good man are
ordered by the LORD ; and He delighteth
in His way. 24. Though he fall, he shall
not be utterly cast down : for the LORD
upholdeth him with his hand, 25. I have
been young, and now am old ; yet have I
not seen the righteous forsaken, nor his
seed begging bread.' As we came to
this verse, I chanced to look up from my
book toward the swarm of black-coated
pensioners, and amongst them—amongst
them—sat Thomas Newcome." The noble
old man had come to end his days here,
and we know of no chapter in English
literature more affecting than that in which
his light is put out, and he softly murmurs
Adsum.

Tears often refuse to flow when manhood has blunted the sympathies, and we are unmoved when we read again the books which summoned copious floods in youth, but the pathos of Colonel Newcome's death, never loses its effect ; it is so deep and genuine, that the description starts our grief anew whenever we read it, and it leaves us with an acute sense of profound bereavement. We feel a tender interest in the poor brothers, and a high respect for them, because the Colonel was one of them, and because Thackeray, in his imperishable prose, has made them representative of honorable but unfortunate old age.*

* One day, while the great novel of *The New-comes* was in course of publication, Lowell, who was then in London, met Thackeray in the street. The novelist was serious in manner, and his looks and voice told of weariness and affliction. He saw

Charterhouse is the centre of a neighbourhood which Dickens chose for many
of his scenes, as the reader of this knows.
"Only a wall," says Thackeray, in *Mr.
and Mrs. Frank Berry*, "separates the
playground, or 'green,' as it was called
in his time, from Wilderness Row and
Goswell street. Many a time have I
seen Mr. Pickwick look out of his
window in that street, though we did not

the kindly inquiry in the poet's eyes, and said,
"Come into Evans's, and I'll tell you all about it.
I have killed the Colonel!" So they walked in, and
took a table in a remote corner, and then Thackeray, drawing the fresh sheets of MS. from his breast
pocket, read through that exquisitely touching
chapter, which records the death of Colonel Newcome. When he came to the final *Adsum,* the
tears which had been swelling his lids for some
time, trickled down his face, and the last word was
almost an inarticulate sob."—F. H. UNDERWOOD,
in *Harper's Magazine.*

at la fête.

and tenderest tender. Elliot & Clair and the nurse were in the room with him: the latter came to us who were sitting in the adjoining apartment — Madame de Florac was there, with my wife and Bayham.

By the look in the woman's face Madame de Florac started up—

"He is very bad, he murmurs a great deal, the nurse whispered. The Chaplain bids the girl ... that time. The French lady felt curiously, on her knees, and murmured liquid in prayer.

Some ... afterwards Ethel came in with a scared face to our party. He is calling for you again dear Lady — going up to Madame de Florac who was still kneeling. And just now he said he wanted Pendin... his to take care of his boy. He bids not know you? She led her tears as she spoke.

We went into the room where Clive was at the beds foot. The old man within it ... ... a ...

... again ... sigh and be still — One more I heard him say hurriedly. ... came & him whom I in ... later. And there with a heard sending ...

... the Chapel bell began to toll, and ...

the last bell struck — a peculiar sweet smile shone over his face, and he lifted up his head a little, and said ... ... and fell back. It was the word we used to ... at School when names were called: a ... he whatever heard was as that of a little child, he answered to his name, and stood in the presence of

The Master.

know him then." Not only of Mr. Pickwick, but of many other characters, do we
find reminiscences in Smithfield. The
Sarah Son's Head, as John Browdy called
it, Snow Hill, Saffron Hill, Fleet Lane,
and Kingsgate street are not far away.
The buildings with the ancient fronts, the
idlers at the corners, and the confusing
little alleys, which lead where no one would
expect them to lead, all belong to Dickens's
London. The miserable associations of his
early life, his interest in the poor, and his
relish for the grotesque, drew him into the
shady and disreputable quarters of the
city ; and the student of his works can
track him with greater ease and ampler
results in neighbourhoods like Smithfield
than in the West End. With Thackeray,
the reverse is the case ; and, excepting
Charter-house, the reader who desires to

identify his localities finds little to reward him in a search east of Pall Mall, or south of Oxford street.

IV.

ON the site of the Imperial Club in Cursitor street, Chancery Lane, stood a notorious "sponging house," to which Rawdon Crawley was taken when arrested for debt, immediately after leaving the brilliant entertainment given by the Marquis of Steyne, and from which he wrote an ill-spelled letter to his wife (who had appeared triumphantly in some charades at that entertainment), begging her to send some money for his release. The reader remembers how the faithless little woman answered,—assuring him of her grief and anxiety, and telling him that she had not

the money, but would get it ; though, as
poor, blundering, soft-hearted Rawdon discovered afterward, she had a very large
sum at the moment she wrote to him, and
did not send him any of it because she
wished to keep him in jail that she might
intrigue with the licentious old marquis ;
and the reader will remember that Rawdon
was released at the instance of his cousin's
wife, and went to the little house in Curzon
street, where he surprised his deceitful
spouse, and nearly murdered her companion, the same old Marquis of Steyne,
knight of the garter, lord of the powder-
box, trustee of the British Museum, etc.

When we come to the end of that passage, we put the book on our lap and lean
back in the chair, and, while we are still
glowing with the excitement of the scene,
we are filled with admiration of the genius
which produced it. How did Thackeray

achieve his effects? Becky Sharp is a
unique and permanent figure in literature,
a subtle embodiment of duplicity, ambition,
and selfishness. She is avaricious, hypo-
critical, specious, and crafty. Though not
malignant nor to a certainty criminal, she
is a conscienceless little malefactor, whose
ill deeds are only limited by the ignoble
dimensions of her passions. She lies with
amazing glibness, is utterly faithless to her
hulking husband, and utterly indifferent to
her child. Her mendacity is superlative,
and double-dealing enters into all her
transactions. But she is so shrewd, so
vivacious, so artful, so immensely clever and
good-humoured, she has so much prettiness
of manner and person, that, while we des-
pise her, and have not the least pity for
her when retribution falls heavily upon her,
our indignation against her is not so great
as we feel that it ought to be, principally

because her sins have a certain feminine
archness and irresponsibility in them, which
keeps them well down to the level of
comedy.   When we close the book we
know her through and through, and
thoroughly understand all the complex
workings of her strategic mind.   How do
we know her so well?   Thackeray is not
exegetical, and does not depend on elaborate analysis for his effects.   The actions
of the characters are themselves fully ex-
pository, and do not call for any outside
comments or enlargement on the part of
the author.   This is the case to such an
extent that, when we examine the com-
pleteness with which the characters are
revealed to us, we are inclined to believe
that Thackeray's art is of the very highest
kind, and that, though in form it is
undramatic, intrinsically it is powerfully
dramatic.

But we are straying from our purpose, which is simply to look for ourselves at the places which he has described. Across the way from the bottom of Chancery Lane is the Temple, to the interest of which he has added many associations. He was fond of its dark alleys, archways, courts, and back stairs.

In 1834 he was called to the bar, and for some time he occupied chambers in the venerable buildings with the late Tom Taylor. His rooms, which were at number 10 Crown Office Row, have disappeared before "improvements" that present a modern front to the gardens and the river. Philip had chambers in the Temple, and there, also, in classic Lamb's Court, Pendennis and Warrington were located.

Warrington smoking his cutty pipe, and writing his articles—the fine-hearted fellow, the unfortunate gentleman, the unpedantic

scholar, who took Pendennis by the hand
and introduced him to Grub street when
that young unfortunate came to the end of
his means. George Warrington teaches us
a new lesson in manhood, in patience, in
self-abnegation. His lot is full of sorrow,
his cherished ambitions are impossible,
through no fault of his own, but it is not
in him to surrender to "the dull gray life
and apathetic end,"—his contentment is the
repose of a generous nature, his cheeriness
with his pipe and his work springs out of
a calmly philosophic mind, a satisfied con-
science, a profound faith, and when we
pass through Lamb's court, not least in our
affections is the shadow of him.

"The man of letters cannot but love
the place which has been inhabited by
so many of his brethren, and peopled
by their creations as real to us at this
day, as the authors whose children they

were," and says Thackeray, "Sir Roger de Coverley walking in the Temple garden, and discoursing with Mr. Spectator about the beauties in hoops and patches who are sauntering over the grass, is just as lively a figure to me, as old Samuel Johnson rolling through the fog with the Scotch gentleman at his heels, on their way to Mr. Goldsmith's chambers in Brick court, or Harry Fielding, with inked ruffles and a wet towel round his head, dashing off articles at midnight for the *Covent Garden Journal,* while the printer's boy is asleep in the passage."

Leaving the Temple, we once more enter Smithfield, to look for the site of the old Fleet prison, the scene of many episodes in the stories of Dickens. It was in this strange place, that the brilliant, but thriftless Captain Shandon lived, "one of the wisest, wittiest, and most incorrigible of

Irishmen ; " here Pendennis found him sitting on a bed, in a torn dressing gown,
with a desk on his knees : here a prisoner
for debt, he indited the prospectus of the
Pall Mall Gazette, which was so called,
he said, because its editor was born in
Dublin, and the sub-editor (excellent Jack
Finucane) at Cork ; because the proprietor
lived in Paternoster Row, and the paper
was published in Catherine Street, Strand.
This imaginary title of Thackeray's was
not the only one afterwards adopted
by a real newspaper.   He writes of the
Whitehall Review as an opposing print,
and that is now the name of a successful
London journal.

The Fleet is a thing of the past, and the
attributes of Captain Shandon have no in-
heritors in the press of to-day.   A knight
armed cap-à-pie in Cheapside, would not
be a more antiquated figure, than the

boozy scholar editing a reputable journal
in the cell of a prison. Journalism has
taken off its soft hat and shabby clothes ;
it has mended its erring and improvident
ways, and put on the manners of polite
society. Not in a tap-room, with jorums
of hot whiskey, Welsh rabbits, and devilled
chops does the modern scribe regale himself. He has a club somewhere in Adelphi,
or St. James', where he presents himself
in sedate evening dress, he turns pale at
the very mention of supper, and, instead
of singing old English songs, sadly com-
pares notes with his fellow-dyspeptics. A
vulgar public-house, or low music hall stands
on the site of the Haunt and the Back
Kitchen. When Warrington, Pendennis,
Tom Sarjeant, Clive Newcome, and Fred.
Bayham frequented the Haunt, and joined
in the diversions of the literary democracy,
there was a superstition among them, that

the place vanished at the approach of day-
break, that when Betsy turned the gas off
at the door lamp, as the company went
away, the whole thing faded into mist—
the door, the house, the bar, Betsy, the
beer-boy, Mrs. Nokes, and all. Whether
this was so or not, it has now vanished, not
for a day, but for ever, like Captain Shandon, and the wild Bohemianism of his
time.*

* Mr. Edmund Yates states in his interesting
Memoirs of a Man of the World, that the Cider
Cellars, next to the stage door of the Adelphi, was
the prototype of the Back Kitchen, immortalized in
Pendennis. The Cave of Harmony, frequently
mentioned by Thackeray, was sketched from
Evans's, in Covent Garden.

V.

IT is only a minutes' walk from the corner of Fleet Lane, to the street of booksellers, Paternoster Row, in which the rival publishers, Bungay and Bacon lived—Bacon in an ancient low-browed building, with a few of his books displayed in the windows under a bust of my Lord Verulam; and Bungay in the house opposite, which was newly painted, and elaborately decorated in the style of the seventeenth century, "so that you might have fancied stately Mr. Evelyn passing over the threshold, or curious Mr. Pepys examining the books in the windows." *The* Row, so called—as

financiers arrogantly call Wall Street, *the*
Street—is not wider than an alley way, and
in this respect it is exactly as it was when
Warrington introduced Pendennis to the
editor of the *Parlor Table Annual,* wherein
his verses were published. But though its
breadth has not been increased, the old
buildings on both sides of it have given
place in many instances to towering new
ones, five and six stories high, which shut
out the light, and keep the editors, com-
pilers, printers, engravers, and book-binders,
who are the principal laborers of the Row,
in an all-day gloom. Both Bungay and
Bacon had their domestic establishments
over their shops, and their wives, who were
sisters, thus had an opportunity to insult
one another by looks and mute signs from
their opposite windows. Bungay and
Bacon, and their belligerent spouses are
now out of the trade, and the annual

Souvenirs and *Keepsakes* which made a part of their business, belong to an extinct form of literature. The Row is full of Grub Street curiosities; but Lady Fanny Fantail, Miss Bunion, and the Honorable Percy Popinjay are seen within its precincts no more, and if they still exist, they probably find a new field for their distinguished services in the society papers.

Let anyone strike out which way he will from Fleet Street, he is sure to find himself in the presence of something which reminds him of Dickens, near some object which his humor has made famous, or which answers to one of his luminous descriptions.

The slums between the Strand and Soho, and between Smithfield and Clerkenwell, were fertile to him, and not a *gamin* there knew the winding alleys, and crisscross streets better than the gentleman

with the high complexion, the sparkling
eye, the iron-gray beard, the well-cut dress,
and the brisk step, who might have been
seen speeding through them at all sorts of
unusual hours. One day, he was heard of
in Ratcliff Highway, or among the river-
side shanties of Poplar, and the next,
among the bird shops of Seven Dials, or
in the courts of Lambeth. When we con-
trast the little we have found of Thackeray
in the neighbourhood through which we
have just been, with the variety and sugges-
tiveness of the reminiscences of Dickens in
the same region, our search seems dis-
appointing.

As we have said Thackeray was not a
novelist of low life. "Perhaps," he says in
the preface to *Pendennis* : "the lovers of
excitement may care to know that this
book began with a very precise plan, which
was entirely put aside. Ladies and Gen-

tlemen, you were to have been treated, and
the writer's and publisher's pocket bene-
fited by the recital of the most active hor-
rors. What more exciting than a ruffian
(with many admirable virtues) in St. Giles,
visited constantly by a young lady from
Belgravia ? What more stirring than the
contrasts of society ? The mixture of slang
and fashionable language ? The escapes,
the battles, the murders ? . . . . The
exciting plan was laid aside (with a very
honorable forbearance on part of the publishers) because on attempting it, I found
that I failed from want of experience of
my subject ; and never having been intimate with any convict in my life, and the
manners of ruffians and gaol-birds being
quite unfamiliar to me, the idea of entering
into competition with M. Eugene Sue was
abandoned."

—oo;¤;oo—

VI.

THOUGH in the east end of the town and in the south, Thackeray has left few footsteps for us to follow, in ancient and comfortable Bloomsbury, and the region to the west of it and north of Oxford street (called De Quincey's step-mother), we find much to remind us of him. It was in Russell Square that the Sedleys lived in the time of their prosperity, and thence, on the evening after the arrival of gentle Amelia from the boarding school at Chiswick, a messenger was sent for George Osborne, whose house was No. 96. Russell Square is the largest and handsomest of the chain

RUSSELL SQUARE, WHERE THE SEDLEYS LIVED

of squares which extend, almost without a
break, from Oxford street to the New Road
—Bloomsbury Square, Woburn Square,
Gordon Square, Tavistock Square, and
Euston Square. The neighbourhood has
seen many strange shifts of fortune, and
some of the finest of its mansions are de-
based to the uses of common boarding-
houses and private hotels. There are streets
and streets of houses with white cards in
the windows announcing "Lodgings to let."
Sombre old houses they are, built of brick,
with flat, uninteresting fronts, the sooty
darkness of which is sometimes relieved by
a yellowish portico, freshly painted, or a
plaster shell of a drab colour reaching from
the basement to the second story. The
cheeriness of the spreading trees in the
little parks, the flowering shrubs, the
shining fountains, and the grass, are only
a partial alleviation. Russell Square has

deteriorated less than some of the other
places in the neighbourhood, however, and
the houses around it would not be beneath
the inclinations of a prosperous merchant
such as old Sedley was. We look in vain
for 96 ; the numbers do not go as high as
that ; but we have no difficulty in singling
out the respectable dwelling on the western
side in which poor Amelia sighed for her
selfish lover, and Becky Sharp set her cap
at the corpulent Mr. Jos.

How sad the story of the Sedleys is !—
the unrequited love of Amelia—the untime-
ly death of George at Waterloo—the failure
of old Sedley, and the cold-heartedness of
the elder Osborne ! The decayed merchant
musing over all sorts of fatuous schemes
by which he hopes to recover his position,
and sitting in the dark corner of a coffee-
house with his letters spread out before
him—letters relating to a make-believe and

visionary business—which he is anxious to
read to every friend, is the most touching
picture, after the death of Colonel Newcome, which Thackeray has drawn.

"What guest at Dives's table can pass
the familiar house without a sigh ?—the
house of which the lights used to shine
so cheerfully at seven o'clock—of which
the hall doors opened so readily—of which
the obsequious servants, as you passed
up the comfortable stairs, sounded your
name from landing to landing, until it
reached the apartment where jolly old
Dives welcomed his friends ! What a
number of them he had ! What a
noble way of entertaining them ! . . .
How changed is the house, though ! The
front is patched over with bills, setting forth
the particulars of the furniture in staring
capitals. They have hung a shred of car-
pet out of the upstairs window—a half

dozen of porters are lounging on the dirty
steps—the hall swarms with dingy guests
of oriental countenance, who thrust printed
cards into your hands, and offer to bid. Old
women and amateurs have invaded the
upper apartments, pinching the bed cur-
tains, poking the feathers, shampooing the
mattresses, and clapping the wardrobe
drawers to and fro. . . O Dives, who
who would have thought, as we sat round
the broad table sparkling with plate and
spotless linen, to have such a dish at the
head of it as that roaring auctioneer?"

Among the bidders was a six-foot, shy-
looking military gentleman, who bought a
piano, and sent it without any message to
the little house—St. Adelaide Villa, Anna
Maria Road, West—to which the Sedleys
had retired after their downfall, and there,
as the reader no doubt remembers, Amelia
received it with great gladness, believing

that it came from her well-beloved George. It was years before she discovered that it was not her faithless lover, but simple, brave, tender-hearted Captain Dobbin, to whom she should have been grateful.

It was in Hart street, two blocks nearer Oxford street than Russell Square, that little George Osborne went to school at the house of the Rev. Laurence Veal, domestic chaplain to the Earl of Bareacres, who prepared young noblemen and gentlemen for the universities, the senate, and the learned professions, whose system did not embrace the degrading corporal severities still practiced at the ancient places of education, and in whose family the pupils found the elegancies of refined society, and the confidence and affection of a home. Thither came poor Amelia, walking all the way from Brompton to catch a glimpse of her darling boy, who had been taken away from her by his obdurate grandfather.

Great Russell street is next to Hart
street, and on it fronts the classic portico of
the British Museum, in the splendid read-
ing-room of which Thackeray was often
seen. It was in Great Coram street, adjoining the celebrated foundling hospital,
that he lived, when, one evening, he called
on a young man who had chambers in
Furnival's Inn, and offered to illustrate the
works which were beginning to make "Boz"
famous ; and we can see him coming back
to his lodgings in low spirits over the rejec-
tion of his proposal, for at that time
Thackeray was poor, and neither literature
nor art, which he loved the better, would
support him.

About half a mile farther north, across
Tottenham Court Road, is Fitzroy Square ;
and when we look for 120, we find that 40
is the highest number which the Square
includes. Though the little circular garden

DOOR-WAY OF 37 FITZROY SQUARE, WHERE
NEWCOME LIVED.

which it incloses is prettily laid out, and is
one of the leafiest of the oases between
Euston and Bloomsbury, Fitzroy has
degenerated more than some of the other
squares in the neighborhood. It was not very
fashionable when Colonel Newcome took
No. 120 with James Binnie, and it is not
fashionable at all now. One side is badly
out of repair. There are two or three
doctors' houses in it, several houses with
announcements of apartments to let, and a
private hotel. The particular house occupied by the Colonel and his old Indian
friend cannot be easily identified by
Thackeray's description. "The house is
vast, but, it must be owned, melancholy.
Not long since, it was a ladies' school in an
unprosperous condition. The scar left by
Madame Latour's brass plate may still be
seen on the tall black door, cheerfully
ornamented in the style of the end of the

last century, with a funereal urn in the
centre of the entry and garlands, and the
skulls of rams at each corner." We fancy
that it was on the south side of the square,
near the middle of a row of heavy sepulchral houses built of stone, which, first
blackened by the London smoke, have
since been unevenly calcined by the at-
mosphere, so that, as in many other
buildings, they look as if a quantity of dirty
whitewash had been allowed to trickle
down them. Some of the ornaments have
been removed, but the urn is still over the
door.

The days spent here were the happiest
in the lives of the good old Colonel and
his son. The Colonel had just returned
from India full of honors and riches, and
with his old chum, James Binnie, he kept
house with lavish hospitality, and much
originality. "The Colonel was great at

making hot-pot, curry, and pillau," Pendennis tells us. " What cozy pipes did we not smoke in the dining-room, in the drawing-room, or where we would ! What pleasant evenings did we not have with Mr. Binnie's books and Schiedam ! Then there were solemn state dinners, at most of which the writer of this biography had a corner." The guests at these entertainments were not selected for their social position or their worldly prosperity, and it mattered not whether they were rich or poor, well dressed or shabby, if they were friends. Old Indian Officers were among them, and young artists with unkempt ways from Newman street and Berners street ; the genial **F. B.** waltzed with elderly houris and ₂ paid them compliments ; Professor Gandish talked about art with many misplaced h's, and the Rev. Charles Honeyman sighed and posed and meekly received the adulation of the women.

Despite the failure of the Bundlecomb Bank, the later part of the history of the Newcomes would have been less sad but for that accident to Mr. Binnie, in which he fell from his horse and was so much injured that Mrs. Mackenzie—the "awful" campaigner—was called in to nurse him with the aid of poor little Rosey. Fitzroy Square is so old that its gloomy houses must have known much sorrow ; but we doubt if any of them has seen anything more pitiable than the humiliation of Colonel Newcome, or anything crueller than the remorseless tyranny of the "campaigner" and her fierce temper—the "campaigner," who was all smiles, coquetry, and amiability, until prosperity fled from those who had been her benefactors, when she suddenly revealed all the pettiness and harshness of her termagant soul.

Three streets away from the Square is Howland street, to which Clive removed with his weak little wife and his spiteful mother-in-law when disaster fell upon him ; and every reader of Thackeray will remember how Pendennis, Clive, and Boy went out to meet the broken-hearted old man as he came along Guilford street and Russell Square, from the Charterhouse to eat his last Christmas dinner.

When we close the history of Colonel Newcome we ask ourselves if any man who moves our hearts as Thackeray does, could be a cynic? Cynicism is a withering of the heart, the exhaustion of a shallow moral nature, the self-consciousness of an ignoble mind. But what pathos is so spontaneous, so genuine, so lasting as Thackeray's—so free from the literary trickery which may

produce tears in youth, but only provokes
a smile when age has dulled the feelings
and opened the eyes to artifice. Among
all English authors the writer of this little
book, at least, does not recognize one who
is more unaffectedly tender than this great
social preacher, who speaks with unflinching
candour of evil, but glorifies all good, and
reads with unfeigned pity the lessons of
life.

VII.

BEFORE Thackeray died, he had become as familiar a figure in the West End of London as Dr. Johnson was in Fleet street and its tributary courts and lanes. Any one who did not know him might have supposed him to be an indolent man about town; and those who could identify him generally knew where to find him, if they wished to show the great author to a friend from the country. He was usually present in the Park at the fashionable hour; and if the Pall Mall of his day is ever painted, his face and form will be as inseparable from a truthful picture as the mammoth bulk of

.the testy lexicographer is from the contemporaneous prints of old Temple Bar.

Pall Mall is the street of gentlemen, as Fleet Street was the street of the ragged literary mendicants, whose wretched lot has been drawn in vivid colours by Macauley. The people one meets in it are daintily booted, gloved and hatted ; a lady is not often seen among them. It is, as Thackeray himself said, " the social exchange of London :" the main artery of Clubland, where civilized man has set up for himself all the adjuncts of luxurious celibacy, and congregates to discuss, undisturbed by the impertinencies of feminine lack-logic, the news, the politics and the scandal of the hour. It is old and historic, haunted by the shadows of many odd and famous persons, who reshape themselves unbidden in the memory of those who know its annals. The reminiscences bring out a motley

tenancy from the houses —Culloden,
Cumberland and Gainsborough side by
side, pretty Eleanor Gwynn and Queen
Caroline, Sarah Marlborough and genial
Walter Scott, George Selwyn and Dick
Steele, Sheridan and William Pitt, Walpole
and Joseph Addison, and Fox and the
Prince Regent! The greensward at the
south end of the Athenæum Club was a
part of the site of Carlton House, the
residence of the royal scapegrace, and
we see Thackeray, as he has described
himself, a frilled and petticoated urchin
in his nurse's care, peeping through the
colonnade at the guards, as they pace before
the palace, and salute the royal chariots
coming in and out. Before he reached
manhood the palace had disappeared, and
many of the old buildings in Pall Mall had
been pulled down to make room for the
magnificent club houses, which now give

the street its distinctive character.   Not
one of the new faces that appeared with the
alterations was more familiar to the men of
his time than his, and among all the
princes, dandies, politicians, and scholars
who filed through the street and nodded to
one another from their club windows, there
was not one to whom the reading part of
this generation reverts with greater fondness
than to Thackeray.

Those who appreciate his books—a constantly increasing number—find it difficult
to understand how the author can be so
misinterpreted as to be accused of any
narrowness of view or harshness of judgment.   To them every line is testimony of
a fatherly tenderness which grieves at the
necessity of its own rebuke, and though he
is incapable of an apathetic acquiescence
in human weakness, and does not view
mankind with the lazy good nature of a

neutral temper, the pervading spirit of his criticism springs from a deep-welled charitableness.

One of the few stories told of him which would dispute his invariable kindliness is of two friends who were walking in the West End when they saw Thackeray approaching them from the opposite direction. One of them had met him before, and the other had not. The former made a demonstrative salutation, which the author barely acknowledged as he loftily passed along. "You wouldn't believe that he sat up with us drinking punch and singing *Dr. Martin Luther* until three o'clock this morning," said the person, who felt aggrieved at his chilling reception, to his friend. Now supposing that the story is authentic—that two friends did meet him under those circumstances, and that one of them had been a sharer of his conviviality in the small

hours, a further claim on his recognition
was not necessarily justified, and he did
not violate any rule of good breeding in
discouraging it. But there are some who
feel emboldened by the smallest politeness
of a great man to consider themselves
intimate with him, and who once having
seen him come down from his pedestal to
smoke a cutty pipe in a miscellaneous
company ever afterwards look upon him as
a comrade.

The loveableness of his character is well
remembered at the Athenæum Club, and
the old servants, especially, speak of his
kindness to them.   The club house is at the
corner of Waterloo Place and Pall Mall—
a drab-coloured, sedate, classic building,
with a wide frieze under the cornice—in a
line with the Guards, the Oxford and Cam-
bridge, the Reform, the Traveller's, and
many other clubs.   Opposite to it is the

United Service Club, midway is the memorial column to the Duke of York, and only
a few yards away are Carlton Terrace and
the steps leading into St. James's Park.
Marlborough House, the home of the Prince
of Wales, and unpalatial St. James's Palace,
are close by.

Thackeray's name appears on the roll of
the Athenæum as that of a barrister ; but he
was elected in 1851 as "author of *Vanity
Fair*, *Pendennis*, and other well-known
works of fiction."

He was elected under Rule II., which
is worth quoting, as it is designed to
preserve the character of the Club. "It
being essential to the maintenance of the
Athenæum, in conformity with the princi-
ples upon which it was originally founded,
that the annual introduction of a certain
number of persons of distinguished eminence in Science, Literature or the Arts, or

for Public Services, should be secured, a
limited number of persons of such qualifi-
cations shall be elected by the Committee.
The number so elected shall not exceed
Nine each year . . . The Club intrust
this privilege to the Committee, in the
entire confidence that they will only elect
persons who have attained to distinguished
eminence in Science, Literature, or the
Arts, or for Public Services."

He used the club both for work and
pleasure, and there are two corners of the
building to which his name has become
attached, on account of his association with
them. The dining-room is on the first
floor, at the left-hand side of the spacious
entrance; and he usually sat at a table
in the nearest corner, where the sun
shines plenteously through the high windows, and makes rainbows on the white
cloth in striking the glasses. Theodore

Hook had used the same table, and un-
corked his wit with his wine at it; but it
was in a kindlier strain than the author of
Jack Brag was capable of that Thackeray
enlivened the friends who gathered around
him.

From the Club window he probably saw
many of his own characters going along
Pall Mall: little Barnes Newcome; Fred
Bayham, with his big whiskers; cumbrous
Rawdon Crawley; the sinister Marquis of
Steyne; stylish little Foker; neat Major
Pendennis; homely William Dobbin, and
the dashing Dr. Brand Firmin, as he drove
up or down the Haymarket to or from Old
Parr street. Most of them belonged to the
fashionable or semi-fashionable world, and
the men were sure to be members of some
of the clubs in this neighbourhood. No
doubt he also saw Arthur Pendennis, Clive
Newcome, and Philip Firmin; but it is

likely that they appeared with the greatest
distinctness when the blinds were drawn
and the reflection of his own face was visible
in the darkened windows.

He was a *bon vivant:* fond of a nice
little dinner, a connoisseur of wines, the
devotee of a good cigar, a willing receiver
of many little pleasures which an ascetic
judgment would pronounce wasteful and
slothful. He was inclined to be indolent
and luxurious. Had he not lost his fortune,
and been urged by necessity to write, it is to
be feared that his splendid gifts would never
have been exercised, and that his genius
would have borne no more fruit than an
unworked store of unformulated and un-
analysed mental impressions, known only
to himself. But his liking for choice little
dinners was not wholly accountable to his
relish of the food or to the satisfaction of
thus gratifying the senses. No reproach of

excess or grossness of any kind attaches to his character. Though perhaps he was self-indulgent, he was not a voluptuary. His pleasure was as innocent as that of Colonel Newcome when he visited the smoky depths of Bohemia with young Clive, and the dinner was but the means of sociability and hospitality, the preparation for a more intellectual treat, a key to the fetters which keep some hearts and minds in this oddly-constituted and misgiving world from the openness and confidence of brotherhood.

It was not a cold or formal honour that was conferred upon those who sat with him. When they were taken into his confidence, no friend could be more jovial or unrestrained than he was. The simplicity of the man was one of his greatest charms. He could not endure affectations and mannerisms. He talked without effort, with-

out hesitation, and without any of the
elaborateness which comes of egotistic
cogitation, and the desire to present oneself
in the most favourable light. He was one
of the most " natural " of men, if the word
is taken as meaning the absence of self-
disguise ; and at these little dinners and in
the smoke-room, figuratively speaking, he
usually had his slippers on, and his feet
stretched out on the hearth-rug.*

* " One day, many years ago, I saw him chaffing
on the sidewalk in London, in front of the Athenæum Club, with a monstrous-sized, ' copiously
ebriose' cabman, and I judged from the driver's
ludicrously careful way of landing the coin deep
down in his breeches-pocket, that Thackeray had
given him a very unusual fare. ' Who is your fat
friend ?' I asked, crossing over to shake hands with
him. ' O ! that indomitable youth is an old crony
of mine,' he replied ; and then, quoting Falstaff, ' a
goodly portly man, i' faith, and a corpulent, of a
cheerful look, a pleasing eye, and a most noble car-

very faithfully yours

W M Thackeray

ENGRAVED BY W. B. CLOSSON, FROM A DAGUERREOTYPE TAKEN BY BRADY DURING THACKERAY'S VISIT TO

The modern smoking-room of the Club
is under the garden, upon which the dining
room of Carlton House once stood ; but in
Thackeray's time a very small apartment
near the top of the building, served for
those addicted to the dreamy weed, and he
was among them.   He was not a great
smoker, though he usually had a cigar at
hand ; he coquetted with it, puffed at it
awhile and watched the blue wreaths van-
ishing towards the ceiling, and then put it
down, or let it go out. He did not apply himself to it with the constancy and caressing
intentness of complete enjoyment, but was

riage.' It was the *manner* of saying this, then and
there, in the London street, the cabman moving
slowly off on his sorry vehicle, with one eye (an eye
dewy with gin and water, and a tear of gratitude,
perhaps) on Thackeray, and the great man himself
so jovial and so full of kindness ! "—*Yesterdays
with Authors.* J. T. FIELDS.

fitful, as if the pleasure he derived was dubious.

Much of the pleasure of his life was dubious. We have here seen but one side of his character, the geniality which was unextinguished by an inherent sadness of temperament : the comfortableness of his hours of relaxation. But he was not a happy man, even when he had achieved success, and his powers had been fully recognized. Self-confidence is an ingredient of genius which was lacking in him. He was always in doubt about his work, he trusted his judgment when he discovered defects in it, but never felt sure of its merits. More distressing than all else was his procrastination : the heart-breaking and peace-destroying spectre of postponed work was too often before him, and he was often crippled by his hesitation and despair.

The south-west corner of the South

library, on the second floor of the Club, is
filled with books of English history, and
some of his work was done there. There-
from, no doubt, some of the material of the
lectures on the Georges was drawn; he
could look out of the window on the very
site of Carlton House, now a square of
grass and flowers; and probably on these
shelves he found some help in com-
pleting *Esmond* and developing *The
Virginians.* He often left the library
looking fatigued and troubled, and he was
sometimes heard complaining of the per-
plexity he found in disposing of this character or that, and asserting that he knew that
what he was writing would fail.

He divided his time between the Athenæum Club, the Reform, and the Garrick.
Contiguous to the first two is the neighborhood of St. James's, which principally con-
sists of clubs, bachelors' chambers, and

fashionable shops, and is associated with
many of Thackeray's characters. At No. 88
St. James's street, in a building now demolished, he himself once occupied chambers,
and there began and finished *Barry Lyndon.*
Major Pendennis had chambers in Bury
street, a narrow lane coming from Piccadilly
parallel with St. James's street ; and it was
in them that the famous scene took place
between the shrewd old soldier and Mr.
Morgan, in which that rebellious flunky
was brought whining to his knees by the
strategic courage of his master. We have
searched the neighbourhood for the "Wheel
of Fortune" public-house, which Mr. Morgan frequented to discuss with other
gentlemen's gentlemen, gentlemen's affairs.
It is not to be found ; and Bury street has
scarcely a house in it that looks old enough
to have been the Major's. But St. James's
Church is here--a gloomy old building of

smoky brick with lighter trimmings of
stone ; and the reader may remember how,
one day, Esmond and Dick Steele were
walking along Jermyn street after dinner
at the Guards', when they espied a fair,
tall man in a snuff-coloured suit, with a
plain sword, very sober, and almost shabby
in appearance, who was poring over a folio
volume at a book-shop close by the church ;
and how Dick, shining in scarlet and gold
lace, rushed up to the student and took
him in his arms and hugged him ; and how
the object of these demonstrations proved
to be Addison, who invited Steele and
Esmond to his chambers in the Haymarket,
where he read verses of the *Campaign*
to them, and regaled them with pipes and
Burgundy. I never walk through Jermyn
street, or past the old church, without seeing
these three figures, and they are no more

like shadows than any in the nineteenth century throng which fills the street.

Willis's Rooms, formerly Almack's, are in King street, which is parallel to Jermyn street, and it was in them, that Thackeray gave his lectures.

VIII.

THACKERAY constantly mixes up real with fictitious names in his descriptions. Some disguise was often necessary, and sometimes even compulsory. He could not be as explicit or as literal as Dickens, because most of his characters represented a very different class. The latter could draw in detail the house he selected as most appropriate for the occupation of Sairey Gamp, because the actual tenants were not likely to find him out, or, if they ever read his description, to quarrel with it. But many of the clients whom Thackeray had to provide with dwellings were great people, and

could only be placed in great neighbourhoods, where the houses are large, conspicu-
ous, and easily distinguished. He either
had to omit any descriptive detail, or to
mask the actual place he had in mind by●
locating it in some street or square with a
fanciful name. Any student of his works will
have no difficulty, however, in finding Guant
House, Gaunt Square, and Great Gaunt
street, if he makes a personal search for
them in Mayfair, though they are not indicated in any map or directory.

Mayfair (let me say for the benefit of
my readers who are so unfortunate as
not to know London) is one of the three
most fashionable neighbourhoods of the
great metropolis, and of the three it is
the most aristocratic and most ancient.
It is, as nearly as possible, a square, about
half a mile wide and three-quarters of a
mile long, bounded at one end by Oxford

street, with its shops and plebeian traffic, at the other end by the most delightful of London streets, Piccadilly ; at one side by Bond street, and at the other by Park Lane, the houses in which overlook the beautiful expanse of Hyde Park. The names of some of its streets have become synonymous with patrician pomp and the affluence of inheritance. It is the highest heaven of social aspiration, the most exalted object of worldly veneration. This is the house of the Duke of Hawksbury ; this of the Earl of Tue-brook ; that of Viscount Wallasey, and that of Lord Arthur Bebbington. It is preëminently the region of the " quality." But let not the reader suppose that it is a region of exterior splendor, of spacious architecture, of brilliant appearance.

Belgravia is far grander to look at, and seems to possess greater riches, and to use

them more lavishly. Even Tyburnia, the
neighborhood to the north of Hyde Park,
is more suggestive of social eminence.
Mayfair displays none of the signs of the
rude enjoyment and proud assertiveness
which spring from recent prosperity. It
is old-fashioned, un-changing, and dull. It
is little different from what it was at the
beginning of the century, except that it is
nearer decay, and that febrile irruptions of
modern Queen Anne architecture occasionally vary the sombreness of its original
style. The physiognomy of its houses ex-
presses a sort of torpor, as if familiarity
with honours were as wearisome as continuous association with misfortune. They
have an air of funereal resignation. Many
of the streets are short and narrow : many
of the houses are dingy. The ornaments
are of a sepulchral kind, such as urns over
the door-ways, and funeral wreaths about

the porticoes. The blazoned heraldry of
the hatchments has been nearly extinguished by the smoke. At some doors
there are two incongruous obelisks, joined
to the iron railing which screens the basement, and the portico is extended to the
curb. But ornaments even as unsatisfac-
tory as these are not common, and most
of the houses, with high fronts of blackened
brick and oblong windows, are unadorned,
except by a few boxes of flowers on the
sills. The lackeys, with crimson knee-
breeches, white stockings, laced coats,
buckled shoes, and powdered hair, blaze
in this gloom with a pyrotechnic splendour.
Occasionally, the uniform rows of smoky
brick and pointed stucco houses are over-
shadowed by a larger mansion, shut within
its own walls, and some of the streets enter
spacious squares, where there are sooty
trees and grass and chirping sparrows.

It is possible that Thackeray had no
exact place in mind when he wrote of
Gaunt House and Gaunt Square, but it
is not likely. The creatures of his imagination were flesh and blood to him, too
vital to be left without habitations. "All
the world knows," he says in *Vanity
Fair*, "that Gaunt House stands in Gaunt
Square, out of which Great Gaunt street
leads. . . . . Gaunt House occupies
nearly a side of the square. The remain-
ing three sides consist of mansions which
have passed away into dowagerism. . . .
It has a dreary look, nor is Lord Steyne's
palace less dreary. All to be seen of it
is a vast wall in front, with rustic columns
at the great gate." Berkeley Square
almost exactly corresponds with this
description. Here are the gloomy mansions, looking out on grass and trees
which seem to belong to a cemetery, and

here, immediately recognizable, is the
palace, filling nearly a side of the square,
and shut within high walls to hide what
they inclose from the prying eyes of the
passers, though the upper stories can be
seen from the opposite side of the way.
Here is the very gate, with heavy knockers,
though the rustic columns of Thackeray's
text have been replaced by new ones of
a different shape. We do not find in the
middle of the square the statue of Lord
Gaunt, "in a three-tailed wig, and other-
wise habited like a Roman emperor," but
we can identify almost every other detail
of the picture. Now, as this palace has
long been occupied by a noble family, it
would not be just for us to mention the
name of the house, lest some undeserved
reproach should thereby fall on the
tenants; for, while Thackeray described
the locality with such faithful elaboration

it is not to be inferred that he drew the character of Lord Steyne from an actual person living in the neighbourhood; nothing indeed, could be less probable.

He also speaks of the square as Shiverley Square, and briefly mentions it in describing Becky's drive to the house of Sir Pitt Crawley : "Having passed through Shiverley Square into Great Gaunt street, the carriage at length stopped at a tall, gloomy house, between two other tall, gloomy houses, each with a hatchment over the middle drawing-room window, as is the custom in Great Gaunt street, in which gloomy locality death seems to reign perpetual."

Great Gaunt street is undoubtedly Hill street, which he mentions specifically in another place as the home of Lady Gaunt's mother. Sometimes it was necessary for him to invent a name, and when he did so

he was peculiarly apt. Gaunt Square seems
a more fitting and descriptive name than
Berkeley Square, but he frequently varied
the real with the fictitious name with play-
ful caprice.

It was in another of these queer old
streets in Mayfair that that wicked old
fairy godmother, the Countess of Kew, lived,
and there (in Queen street) Ethel Newcome
visited her, and was instructed in the ri-
gourous social code which unites fortune
with fortune, or fortune with rank, and
which is by no means limited to Mayfair
or Belgravia, but finds expositors and ad-
herents under the bluer skies of America.
Ethel herself lived with her mother in Park
Lane, the western boundary of Mayfair,
and assuredly the most attractive part of
the region. Park Lane has all of Hyde
Park before its windows, —all the variegated
and plentifully stocked flower-beds of the

Ring Road, the wide sweep of grassy playground, and the knots of patriarchal trees
which give the Park one of its greatest
charms. Unlike most of the region behind
it is cheerful ;   or, if not exactly cheerful,
it has not the mopish signs of withdrawal
from all natural human interests which are
seen in many of the houses in Gaunt
Square and the tributary streets.   Some of
the houses are small, with oriel windows,
and little balconies filled with flower-pots ;
some of them are palatial in size and de-
coration ;   but all of them are fashionable,
and elderly bachelors are known to give
incredibly large prices for the smallest possible quarters under the roof of the meanest
of them.   The exteriors are not of the
sooty brick which characterizes Hill street,
but of plaster, which is annually repainted
in drab or cream colour at the beginning
of each season.   What with the flowers of

the Park and the gardens which lie before
some of the houses, Park Lane seems a
fitting abode for those who are fortunate
both in birth and in wealth ; it is as patrician as any other part of Mayfair, and it
relieves itself of the gloom which seems to
be considered an inevitable accessory of
respectability elsewhere.

In one of these houses—which one it is
not easy to say, as Thackeray has given
us no clue—Lady Ann Newcome lived, and
at it Mrs. Hobson Newcome looked from
afar with an envy which betrayed itself in
her constant reiterations of her contentment
with her own circumstances. Mrs. Hobson
lived in Bryanston Square, a dingily ver-
dant quadrangle north of Oxford street,
near which Clive had a studio ; and J. J.
Ridley, Fred Bayham, Miss Cann, and the
Rev. Charles Honeyman, lodged together
in Walpole street, Mayfair. The Rev.

Charles Honeyman's chapel was close by,
and before the story of *Vanity Fair*,
reached its end there was a charitable lady
in the congregation who wrote hymns and
called herself Lady Crawley, and from
whom William Dobbin and Amelia Sedley,
now united, shrunk as they passed her at
the fancy fair, recognizing in that altered
person the dreadful Becky.

In the eyes of the lover of Thackeray,
no character of history or fiction has lent
more interest to Mayfair than Becky, to
which neighbourhood she came with her
husband some two or three years after their
return from Paris, establishing herself in
"a very small, comfortable house in Curzon street," and demonstrating to the world
the useful and interesting art of living on
nothing a year. There is more than one
small house in Curzon street, but among
them all Becky's is unmistakable. It is

BECKY SHARP'S HOUSE, 22 CURZON STREET.

on the south side of the street, near the
western end, and only a few doors farther
east than the house in which Lord Beacons-
field died. It is four stories and a half
high, and is built of blackish brick like its
neighbours, with painted sills and portico.
Its extreme narrowness, compared with its
height, especially distinguishes it : the front
door, with drab pilasters and a moulded
architrave, is just half its width, and only
leaves room for one parlour window on
the first floor. One can see over the rail-
ings into the basement and through the
kitchen windows. Phantoms appear to us
in all the windows—the ghost of Becky
herself, dressed in a pink dress, her shapely
arms and shoulders wrapped in gauze ; her
ringlets hanging about her neck ; her feet
peeping out of the crisp folds of silk—
"the prettiest little feet in the prettiest
little sandals in the finest silk stockings

in the world." It was in this cozy little
domicile that the arch little hypocrite en_
tertained Lord Steyne, whose house in
Gaunt Square is only a few hundred yards
distant, and Rawdon fleeced young South-
down at cards. No one can help smiling
at the remembrances that come upon him
in looking at those basement windows.
No one who has read *Vanity Fair* is
likely to forget the picture of the sensual
marquis gazing into the kitchen and seeing
no one there just before he knocks at the
door, where he is met by Becky, who is as
fresh as a rose from her dressing-table, and
who excuses her pretended dishabille by
saying that she has just come out of the
kitchen, where she has been making pie,
to which palpable lie the marquis gives an
audacious affirmation by adding that he saw
her there as he came in !

This little house was chosen for that

scene in which Thackeray's genius rises to
its highest point of dramatic intensity; and
so many literary pilgrims come to peep at
it that the tenants must be annoyed, though
the policeman on the beat has become so
accustomed to them that he no longer eyes
them cornerwise or suspects them of bur-
glarious intentions.

IX.

THE places with which Thackeray was personally associated are more interesting, perhaps, than the scenes of his novels. In 1834, he lived in Albion street, near Hyde Park Gardens, and it was there that he, a young man of twenty-three, began to contribute to *Fraser's Magazine*. In 1837, then newly married, he lived in Great Coram street, close by the Foundling Hospital. As I have stated, he had chambers at No. 10, Crown Office Row, in the Temple, and at No. 88, St. James's street, both of which buildings are now demolished. When he had become a successful author, he lived in Brompton and Kensington, and at the latter place, to which he was greatly attached, he died. He was at No. 36, Onslow Square, Brompton, when he unsuccessfully offered himself as member of Parliament for Oxford, and two years later, when he began to discover the thorns in the editorial cushion of the *Cornhill Magazine.* Mr. James Hodder, his private secretary, has given us an interesting glimpse of him as he was while in Onslow Square :—

"Duty called me to his bed-chamber every morning, and as a general rule I found him up and ready to begin work, though he was sometimes in doubt and difficulty as to whether he should commence sitting, or standing, or walking, or lying down. Often he would light a cigar, and, after pacing the room for a few minutes, would put the unsmoked remnant on the mantel-piece and resume his work with increased cheerfulness, as if

he gathered fresh inspiration from the gentle odours
of the sublime tobacco."

Little wonder that he liked Kensington.
It is the pleasantest of the many pleasant
London suburbs. Though it is not four
miles from Charing Cross, to which it is
knitted by continuous streets and houses,
it is like a thriving country town, old-
fashioned, but prosperous, with shops as
brilliant and as well stocked as those of
Regent street, and with many evidences
of antiquity, but none of decay. There are
lofty new buildings and old ones, behind
the modernized fronts of which you can see
leaded dormer windows, angular chimney-
pots, and bowed-down roofs of red tiles.
There are many weather-worn but splendid
mansions shut within their own high walls,
and some in less sequestered gardens. The
place is famous for its fine old trees and
open spaces of verdure. Holland House is

GULIELMO · MAKEPEACE · THACKERAY
CARTHUSIANI · CARTHUSIANO
H · M · P · C
NATUS · MDCCCXI · OBIIT · MDCCCLXIII
ALUMNUS · MDCCCXXII · MDCCCXXVIII

MEMORIAL TABLET TO THACKERAY IN THE CHARTER-HOUSE CHAPEL.

here, and the palace in which Queen Victoria was born, with the beautiful and deeply wooded gardens adjoining Hyde Park. The inhabitants of the old suburb have had many illustrious persons among them ; and Thackeray is one of those best and most affectionately remembered.

His tall, commanding figure was often seen in the old High street, moving along erect, with a firm, stately tread, though his dress was somewhat careless and loose-fitting ; his large, candid face was serious and almost severe as he walked on engaged in meditation, but, being awakened from his reverie by the voice of a friend, a glad smile quickly overspread it and illuminated it. He had many friends among his neighbors, and often sat down to dinner with them. He attended regularly the nine o'clock services in the old parish church on Sunday mornings.

From 1847 to 1853, Thackeray lived in
the bay-windowed house known as the
" Cottage," at No. 13 (now No. 16) Young
street, and in it *Vanity Fair*, *Esmond*
and *Pendennis* were written. There are
few houses in the great city which possess
a more brilliant record than this. Most of
his work was done in a second-story room,
overlooking an open space of gardens and
orchards; and the gentleman who at present
occupies the house has placed an entablature under the window commemorating the
genius that has consecrated it. Between
the dates, 1847 and 1853, the initials
W. M. T. are grouped in a monogram in
the centre of the entablature, and in the
border the names of *Vanity Fair*, *Esmond*, and *Pendennis*, are inscribed.
Just across the street Miss Thackeray
(Mrs. Ritchie) now lives, in full view of
her old home, and in her charming novel *Old*

Kensington, she affectionately calls Young
street "dear old street!" There is no doubt
that the happiest years of Thackeray's life
were spent in the old, bow-windowed cottage.*

I have talked with many persons who
knew him intimately, and under various
circumstances. All speak of him in one
way,—of his gentleness, his kindliness, his
sincerity, and his generosity. "That man
had the heart of a woman!" fervidly said
one who was his next-door neighbour for
several years. This gentleman, Dr. J. J.

* "I once made a pilgrimage with Thackeray (at
my request, of course, the visits were planned) to
the various houses where his books had been written ; and I remember, when we came to Young
street, Kensington, he said, with mock gravity,
'Down on your knees, you rogue, for here *Vanity
Fair* was penned ! And I will go down with you,
for I have a high opinion of that little production
myself.'"—*Yesterdays with Authors.* J. T. FIELDS.

Merriman, whose family have lived in Kensington Square since 1794, possesses a
number of valuable souvenirs of the great
author, including some unpublished letters,
in one of which Thackeray regrets that he
has not seen the doctor for some time, and
characteristically adds: "I wish *Vanity Fair*
were not so big or we performers in it so
busy; then we might see each other and
shake hands once in a year or so." On one
occasion the doctor begged him to write
his name in a copy of *Vanity Fair* which
Thackeray had given him, and the latter
not only did this, but made an exquisite
little drawing on the title-page, than which
the book could not have a more suggestive
or appropriate frontispiece. A little boy
and girl are seated on the ground, one
blowing bubbles and the other hugging a
doll, while behind them looms up the por-
tentous mile-stone of life.

The "dear old street," as Miss Thackeray calls it, ends in Kensington Square, which is full of old houses, to each of which some historic interest belongs. The square was built in the latter part of the seventeenth century, and in one of the old houses Lady Castlewood, Beatrice, and Colonel Esmond lived, and there sheltered the reckless and unscrupulous Pretender.*

In 1853, Thackeray left Kensington and went to live in Onslow Square, Brompton ; but he came back to the old court suburb in 1861, and occupied the fine new house which he had built for himself in the Palace Gardens. It is the second house on the west side of the street, a substantial mansion of red brick, adjoining a much more

---

* Kensington Square has had many celebrated inhabitants, including Talleyrand, Joseph Addison, the Duchess of Mazarin, and Archbishop Herring.

picturesque and older house covered with
ivy ; and it was here that he died suddenly
on December 24, 1863, in the room at the
south-east corner of the second story.
The last time that I saw it, an auctioneer's
flag was hung out, and the broker's men
were playing billiards in the lofty northern
extension which Thackeray built for a
library, and in which he wrote *Denis
Duval.*

Thackeray was buried in Kensal Green
cemetery in the north-west of London, and
was followed to the grave by Dickens,
Browning, Millais, Trollope, and many who
knew the goodness of the soul that had
been called away.   Kensal Green is as un-
attractive as a burial ground could be.   It
is like a prison-yard, with few trees, and
inclosed by high brick walls.   But its nu-
merous tenantry include many who have
worked faithfully and well in literature and

art ; and surrounded by the memorials of
these is one of the simplest tombstones in
the place, inscribed with two dates and the
name of William Makepeace Thackeray.